PRAISE FOR
SJÓN

"[*The Blue Fox*] describes its world with brilliant, precise, concrete colour and detail while at the same time making things and people mysterious and un-graspable . . . The novel is a parable, comic and lyrical, about the nature of things."

—A. S. Byatt, *The Times* (London)

"[*The Blue Fox* is] Sjón's breakthrough work . . . [A] taut, poetic and beautifully judged fable."

—Carolyne Larrington,
The Times Literary Supplement

"Sjón is the trickster that makes the world, and he is ach-ingly brilliant." —Junot Díaz

"Sjón writes like a madman . . . By turns wildly comic and incandescent, elegant and brittle with the harsh

loneliness of a world turned to winter . . . There is no other way to navigate such waters but to dive right in."
—Keith Donohue, *The Washington Post*

"Quirky, melodic, ticklish, seamlessly translated, lovingly polished."
—David Mitchell

"Prismatic: the reader feels that just beneath the surface there are strange and luminous things moving, leaving a series of small hidden detonations."
—Barry Forshaw, *The Independent*

"[Sjón] is a magpie, taking myths and stories from disparate times and places, and weaving them together. The results are not whimsical—Sjón does not shy away from unpleasant truths, either in this world or the realms of myth—and there is a fierce intelligence behind the genial, seemingly rambling narratives."
—Lucy Dallas,
The Times Literary Supplement

THE BLUE FOX

THE BLUE FOX

SJÓN

TRANSLATED FROM THE ICELANDIC BY VICTORIA CRIBB

FARRAR, STRAUS AND GIROUX   NEW YORK

Farrar, Straus and Giroux
18 West 18th Street, New York 10011

Printed in the United States of America
Originally published in Icelandic in 2004 by Bjartur, Iceland,
as *Skugga-Baldur*
English translation originally published in 2008 by Telegram,
Great Britain
Published in the United States by Farrar, Straus and Giroux
First American edition, 2013

Library of Congress Cataloging-in-Publication Data
Sjón, 1962–
    [Skugga-Baldur. English]
    The blue fox / Sjón; translated from the Icelandic by Victoria
Cribb. — 1st American ed.
        p.   cm.
    ISBN 978-0-374-11445-9
    1. Hunters—Iceland—19th century—Fiction.   2. Priests—
Iceland—19th century—Fiction.   3. Down syndrome—Fiction.
4. Natural history—Iceland—19th century—Fiction.   5. Fairy
tales.   6. Mystery fiction.   I. Cribb, Victoria.   II. Title.

PT7511.S62 S5913 2013
839'.6934—dc23

                                                        2012039701

Designed by Jonathan D. Lippincott

www.fsgbooks.com
www.twitter.com/fsgbooks • www.facebook.com/fsgbooks

10 9 8 7 6 5 4 3 2 1

I

(JANUARY 9-11, 1883)

Blue foxes are so curiously like stones that it is a matter for wonder. When they lie beside them in winter there is no hope of telling them apart from the rocks themselves; indeed, they're far trickier than white foxes, which always cast a shadow or look yellow against the snow.

A blue vixen lies tight against her stone, letting the snow drift over her on the windward side. She turns her rump to the weather, curls up, and pokes her snout under her thigh, lowering her eyelids till there's the merest hint of a pupil. And so she keeps an eye on the man who has not shifted since he took cover under the overhanging drift, here on the upper slopes of Asheimar, some eighteen hours ago. The snow has drifted and fallen over him until he resembles nothing so much as a hump of ruined wall.

The creature must take care not to forget that the man is a hunter.

He began his pursuit away south at Botn. The sky was clear and the first blush of day at its winter blackest. The man slid down over the home fields, then set a course north over the Asar to Litla-Bjarg, where it had not drifted as yet.

Once there, he caught a movement on the brow of the hill. Thrusting a hand inside his clothes, he took out a spyglass, extended it, and put it to his good eye:

Yes, there was no mistaking it!

There was a daughter of Reynard on the move.

She seemed blithely unaware of any danger. All her movements indicated that she was on the prowl for a bite to eat. She went about her business unhurriedly, intent on this sole purpose.

The man took a closer look at her.

He bent his thought hard upon her, trying to get an inkling of what she intended, of which way she would go when she had finished her nosing on the crest. All of a sudden she took off at a run; the man couldn't imagine why. Her whole demeanor showed that she sensed a grave threat. Yet she couldn't have had the least suspicion of the man—by ordinary means.

She must have had a foreboding of his intention:

He's a man with hunting on his mind.

The man walked up the hill. He tried to keep the image of the vixen clear in his mind to help him find her again the more easily: "She spins over the hard-packed snow like a top."

Up on the crest he cast around for the vixen's tracks. He pinched one fox print between thumb and forefinger; it seemed a sizable beast. In the snowflake that lingered on his fingertip lay a gleaming hair—there was no mistaking the color: blue.

Vertical streaks of cloud in the west.

Maybe a storm on the way.

The vixen nowhere to be seen.

The trail was plain, as far as the eye could see.

The man walked briskly with the wind at his back. It didn't much matter now if the vixen caught his scent; she knew he was after her.

He paused every now and then to cast around, using the same method as before. He bent all his thought on the one goal of working out which way the vixen would run and where he would get within striking distance.

All at once he receives word of which way she is going and where he will get within striking distance:

"The vixen is going north over the plain. She'll double sharply to the east with the gravel beds of Melar before her, nothing but stones; a perfect hiding place for a blue fox."

Was she too intent to take care? Had she given all her mind over to the danger—thereby letting him into her thoughts? Had she paid no heed to warding him off?

Had the man received a thought-message from the vixen?

Out on the stony plain the air was still and freezing hard; only the lightest breath touched his cheek. The man saw a bluish bump far to the north. He held himself still. After a while the bump began to stir. And shortly afterward a blue vixen rose from the stones.

"Ha, there she is!"

A rare beast. Dark as earth to look at, with a thick pelt and bushy tail, clearly jumpy as hell. She sprang away in sharp, stiff bounds.

The man set off at a run.

As he had suspected, the vixen made straight for the blowing snow. In the very instant before the blizzard swallowed her, she stopped short and glanced back at the man.

Then whisked away again at a terrific pace.

There was a whining in the air.

A ptarmigan hurtled past, a hairsbreadth from the man, driven before the wind. It was followed by a falcon, flying high with sure and steady wing beats.

The man turned away from the blast, tightened his scarf, and wrapped the shoulder strap three times around his right arm so the bag rested tight against his hip.

He was not too late for the storm.

The man trudged through the impenetrable murk.

At first he had stony ground underfoot and the going was not too bad, but the snow soon thickened; conditions deteriorated.

He had to trust to his line of thought:

"The vixen can be childishly weather-shy. She'll dig herself into a drift or press herself deep into crannies, well below the frost mark, and there she'll stay until the foul weather has passed."

Now the man has a chance of lessening the gap between himself and the little fox.

He inched forward.

But just as the man felt he must have gained on the vixen, the snow suddenly deepened. It now came up to his crotch—and with the next step the man sat fast in his tracks.

He could go neither back nor forward; he couldn't see the hand in front of his face.

The blizzard buffeted him from every side, from above and below.

As evening drew on, the weather turned wilder, the frost piercing his clothes in spite of their thickness, and he grew so cold that he had to shiver himself to warmth.

The man decided to let himself be snowed in.

He moved a little while this was happening, so the snow formed a windproof shell around him.

He was of medium stature, stout, and bulky about the chest. His features were coarse; his forehead of middling height but broad, giving his face its character. He had small steel-blue eyes, set deep under heavy brows that met in the middle, and a high-bridged, thick nose. The set of his profile and chin could not be made out for the dark-red beard, shot through with silver, which overlaid cheek and jaw, reaching down to his breast. He had grizzled earth-brown hair. A domed birthmark perched high on his left nostril.

Such was the man in the snowdrift.

The night was cold and of the longer variety.

The man broke off his ice shell.

He praised the Snow Queen and Jack Frost for the shelter they had given him on this fair patch of ground; from this vantage point he could see far and wide over the white frozen wastes.

He now took to pinching and squeezing himself. When he had finished rubbing warmth into the muscles of his upper arms, he pulled on his gloves, braced his hands on the snow ledge, and hoisted himself off his throne.

Yes, he was a lucky dog.

Having shouldered his rifle and bag, the man didn't slow his pace until he reached the smooth rocks of Lofaklopp, those ice-age remnants high up the mountain, where the snow never lies.

There he took off his haversack and removed his gloves, skin shoes, and knitted stockings, laying them to dry on the rock beside him.

No, damn it, he took off every stitch and sat there as he was created: in nothing but his skin.

He was the child of Earth-Sun's daughter.

His guts rumbled and the man discovered that he was hungry; he hadn't tasted a bite since gorging himself on boiled fish before he set off, but that was more than twenty hours ago.

He had eaten a bit of ice since then, truth be told, but that was dull and insubstantial fare. He opened the bag:

Hand-thick slabs of lamb; rye cakes with sheep's butter, sour as gall, topped with mutton sausage; a dried cod's head; pickled blood pudding; dried fish; curd porridge; and a lump of brown sugar.

Yes, all this was in his mess bag.

The sun warms the man's white body, and the snow, melting with a diffident creaking, passes for birdsong.

At noon the peaks were still bright and there were patches of blue in the sky. The man recalled the untold glorious hours he had spent in the mountains since he was a lad. Nothing could equal the beauty of those days—except the new chandelier in the church at Dalbotn.

No! The man flings himself flat on the ground: What did he glimpse there? Was it a boulder?

He grabbed the spyglass but could see nothing. Mist on the lens. He wiped it off with his sleeve. What? Could it be what he thought it was? It vanished, no, there it came back into view:

A fox's head! Yes, the merest shadow of a head. It was the blue. Of course, she must have been on watch there for some time. He closed the spyglass.

The vixen gave a bloodcurdling screech.

The land thereabouts is featureless and slopes to the east, with low tussocks and shallow gullies. There was no way for the man to intercept the vixen without being seen. So he lay still where he had thrown himself when he spotted her. The vixen sprang onto a rock and began to howl. There she sat, pointing her muzzle at the sky every time she uttered a sound.

And so the vixen tried to provoke the man to move. She had probably lost him when he flung himself down.

The man lay flat on his stomach. He had managed to twist himself to face north, with his rifle before him, but didn't dare move because there was no rise in the ground between him and the vixen, nothing to hide him from her view. Moreover, his weapon was not loaded. He couldn't prime it without alerting the little fox.

He had to think fast if he weren't to lose the vixen like the day before—that would be unthinkable.

What was he to do?

The vixen spun around on the rock and poised, ready to vanish. The man rolled over onto his back, waggling arms and legs in the air.

Then he did an about-turn and got on all fours, raising his right leg like a dog pissing on a tussock.

He bleated loudly.

With antics like these the man managed to delay the vixen's departure. He crept into hiding and took thought while she waited for more wonders to appear.

The man loaded his rifle, ramming down half a measure of powder, which would be needed if he were to hit the vixen with his first shot. Putting his hand in his pocket, he fumbled for the tatty little hymnbook he kept there, tore out a page, crumpled it between his fingers, and stuffed it into the barrel. Now it wouldn't whine even if he aimed the weapon straight into the stiff breeze.

He worked quickly, moistening the rifle sight with his spittle and dabbing on a speck of lichen. It froze to the metal, he adjusted it and aimed the rifle experimentally; he would be able to make out the lichen, however dark it got.

The man straightened up and aimed the gun, leaning forward on his left leg, focusing all his attention on the rock. No, the vixen was nowhere to be seen.

He waited for a long time before letting the weapon drop. The vixen wouldn't give him the slip now. Snow covered the land up to the roots of the glacier, not a bare patch of earth to be seen; the vixen would write the tale of her travels on the blank sheet as soon as she embarked on them.

Grasping the weapon in both hands, he set off.

All day long the vixen ran up hill and down dale, the man following hard on her heels.

She was his letter of commission, setting him a task to perform in the material world.

When the man emerged from under the giant boulder that blocks off Asheimar, he came within an inch of losing the vixen.

He just managed to spot her as she turned three circles and flopped against a stone, skulking down and laying her tail over her muzzle.

The man did the same.

The rim of daylight was fading.

In the halls of heaven it was now dark enough for the Aurora Borealis sisters to begin their lively dance of the veils. With an enchanting play of colors they flitted light and quick about the great stage of the heavens, in fluttering golden dresses, their tumbling pearl necklaces scattering here and there in their wild caperings. This spectacle is at its brightest shortly after sunset.

Then the curtain falls; night takes over.

Sleep now became so importunate that the man had never known such overpowering odds. It flashed into his mind that he was in fact dying. He felt weak, his head ached, and his breathing was labored. There was a dull ringing in his ears, yet he could still hear a thudding, a hammering. It was his heart.

What might that bode?

At that very moment the vixen uttered three long-drawn-out warning cries. This was to the east of the man, borne to him on the wind; they struck him like a gust.

He jerked. Darting his eyes to the left, he glimpsed there a blue shape—it seemed to him a devilish coal-black beast.

It vanished.

Dead silence. Not even a heartbeat.

Was he dead, then?

After a considerable time he spied a vixen in the same place as before. She seemed smaller, and all her movements bore witness to exceptional wariness, caution, and cunning. Her behavior was different from before—and she didn't make a sound.

When this one had flaunted herself before the man for a good while, she vanished from view. He fought the yawns that forced their way up to his mouth. Then he became aware of a movement dead ahead; a foxlike form appeared in the night darkness before his eyes. She pirouetted on her hind legs, seemingly free of the earth, coiling like an eel in a river.

A fourth shrieked somewhere out in the night, invisible in the blackness: "Argh, argh!"

The man got a grip on himself. In this part of the coun-try blue foxes were so rare that one alone would be newsworthy. The black one, the shy one, the dancer, and the yelper; they were all the same fox. It could not be otherwise.

"They're all the same fox, all the same fox. They're all the same fox, all the same fox. They're all the same fox, all the same fox . . ."

He repeated the words over and over like a man groping his way out of a nightmare, crying out in his mind. At last he rallied, and when the tears had run from his eyes the man saw that the fox was still in the same place.

And he himself had not moved.

It began to snow.

It snowed.

Blue foxes are so curiously like stones that it is a matter for wonder. When they lie beside them in winter there is no hope of telling them apart from the rocks themselves; indeed, they're far trickier than white foxes, which always cast a shadow or look yellow against the snow.

A blue vixen lies tight against her stone, letting the snow drift over her on the windward side. She turns her rump to the weather, curls up, and pokes her snout under her thigh, lowering her eyelids till there's the merest hint of a pupil. And so she keeps an eye on the man who has not shifted since he took cover under an overhanging drift, here on the upper slopes of Asheimar, some eighteen hours ago. The snow has drifted and fallen over him until he resembles nothing so much as a hump of ruined wall.

The creature must take care not to forget that the man is a hunter.

The fox closes her gray eyes. When she opens them again the man has gone.

She raises her head.

Reverend Baldur Skuggason pulls the trigger.

II

(JANUARY 8-9, 1883)

The world opens its good eye a crack. A ptarmigan belches. The streams trickle under their glazing of ice, dreaming of spring, when they'll swell to a life-threatening force. Smoke curls up from mounds of snow here and there on the mountainsides—these are their farms.

Everything here is a uniform blue, apart from the glitter of the tops. It is winter in the Dale.

"Hello, I've come to fetch the hemale horse, listen, I'm here to take the female porks, oh, eh, no, eh, you, no, hand over the hee-haw forks . . ."

In the yard at Brekka a horse stands beneath a man, and it is the man who is babbling so inanely to himself. He's a big fellow, probably turned forty; there's gray in the pink beard that hangs untrimmed over his mouth and tumbles from his chin like an icebound cataract— yet he is bundled up in clothes like a child all set to spend the day in a snowdrift.

His breeches are hitched right up to his crotch, his coat is far too big or far too small, depending on how you look at it, and his knitted hat is tied so tightly under his chops that he cannot have done it himself; on his hands he wears three pairs of mittens, making it almost impossible for him to hold the reins of the hairy nag on which he sits.

This is the mare Rosa. She champs her bit impatiently. It is her legs that have carried them here. When you look back you can see her hoofprints running from the parsonage at Dalbotn, down over the fields, along the river, across the marshes, up the slopes, to the place where she is now standing, waiting to be relieved of her burden.

Ah, now the man clambers down from her back.

And his true shape is revealed: he is extraordinarily low-kneed, big-bellied, broad-shouldered, and abnormally long-necked, and his left arm is quite a bit shorter than his right. He stamps his feet, beats his arms about himself, shakes his head, and snorts.

The mare flicks her ears.

"Sea-hail porpoise?"

The man scrapes the snow from the farm door with his stubby arm:

"Can it be?"

He knocks on the door with his good hand and feels the blood rushing to his fist. It's cold. Perhaps he'll be invited inside?

The shadow of a man's head appears in the frost-patterned parlor window, and a moment later the inner door can be heard opening, then the front door is thrust out hard. It clears away the pile that has collected outside overnight, and the cold visitor, retreating before it, falls over backward, or would if the snow allowed. When he is done falling, he sees that the man he has come to find is standing in the doorway:

Fridrik B. Fridjónsson, the herbalist, farmer at Brekka, or the man who owns Abba. The visitor's own name is Hálfdán Atlason, "the Reverend Baldur's eejit."

Now he gulps like a fish but says not a word, for before he can recite his piece, Herb-Fridrik invites him to step inside.

And to that the eejit has no other answer than to do as
he is asked.

They enter the kitchen.

"Take off your things."

Fridrik squats, opens the belly of the tiled stove, and
puts in more kindling. It blazes merrily.

It's warm here, a good place to be.

The eejit bites his thumbs and tugs off his mittens
before beginning with trembling hands to struggle with
the tight knot on his hat strings. He's in difficulties, but
his host frees him from his prison. When Fridrik pulls off
his guest's coat a bitter stench is released. Fridrik backs
away, nostrils flaring.

"Coffee . . ."

It was always the same with the Dalbotn folk; they
sweated coffee. The Reverend Baldur was too mean to
give them anything to eat, pumping them instead from
morning to night full of soot-black, stewed-to-pulp coffee
grounds. Fridrik takes a firm hold of Hálfdán's hands;

the tremor that shakes them is not a shiver of cold but a nervous disorder—from coffee consumption.

He releases the man's paws and invites him to sit down. Taking a kettle from a peg, he fills it with melted snow and places it on the hot plate on top of the stove. He points to the kettle and says firmly:

"Now, you keep an eye on the water; when the lid moves come and tell me. I'll be in the parlor, nailing down the coffin lid."

The eejit nods and turns his eyes to the kettle. Herb-Fridrik brushes a hand over his shoulders as he leaves the kitchen. After a moment the sound of hammer blows comes from the next room.

The eejit stares at the kettle and stove in turn, but mostly at the stove. It is a widely famed wonder of technology that few have set eyes on. The metal pipe, which rises from the stove, runs up the wall into the parlor, and from there up to the sleeping loft, warming the house, before poking out through the turf roof and releasing the smoke into the open air. But first and last it is the hand-painted china tiles that enchant: brightly colored flowers sprawl here and there about the body of the stove, nimbler than the eye can follow. Hálfdán rocks in his seat as he traces one flower spray, which winds under this one and over that, all the way up to the kettle.

The kettle, yes, just so, he's keeping an eye on it. The

water spits as it jumps around between the bottom of the kettle and the glowing hot plate.

Fridrik the herbalist is the man who owns his Abba; that is, Hafdís Jónsdóttir, Hálfdán's sweetheart. Fridrik and Abba live together, just the two of them, at Brekka—until she marries Hálfdán, then she'll come away with him. But where might she be today? He twists his elongated neck to peer over his right shoulder.

In the parlor Fridrik is hammering the last nail into the coffin lid. Hálfdán calls in to him:

"I-Hi'm here to fe-fetch the female corpse . . ."

The bleak wording takes Fridrik aback. That's Parson Baldur talking through his manservant. The parsonage servants parroted the priest's mode of speech like a parcel of hens. No doubt one might have called it laughable, had it not been all of a piece, all so ugly and vile.

"I know, Hálfdán, old chap, I know . . ."

But he is even more startled by what the eejit says next:

"Whe-here's h-his A-Abba?"

The water boils and the kettle lid rattles—it sputters slightly at the rim.

"B-boiling," sniffs Hálfdán, and it is the first sound he has uttered since Herb-Fridrik told him that his sweetheart, Abba, was dead, that she was the female corpse the Reverend had sent him to fetch, and that to-day the coffin he saw there on the parlor table would be lowered into the ground in the churchyard at Dalbotn. The news so crushed Hálfdán's heart that he burst into a long, silent fit of weeping and the tears ran from his eyes and nose, while his ill-made body shook in the chair like a leaf quivering before an autumn gale, not knowing whether it will be torn from the bough that has fostered it all summer long or linger there—and wither; but nei-ther fate is good.

While the man grieved for his sweetheart, Fridrik brought out the tea things: a fine hand-thrown English china pot, two bone-white porcelain cups and saucers, a silver-plated milk jug and sugar bowl, teaspoons, and a strainer made of bamboo leaves. And finally a tea caddy made of planed, oiled oak, marked: A. C. PERCH'S THEHANDEL.

He takes the kettle from the hob and pours a little water into the teapot, letting it stand awhile so the china warms through. Then he opens the tea caddy, measures four spoonfuls of leaves into the pot, and pours boiling water over them. The heady fragrance of Darjeeling fills the kitchen, like the steam that rises from newly plowed earth, and there is also a sweet hint, pregnant with sensuality—with memories of luxury—that only one of them has known: Fridrik B. Fridjónsson, the herbalist from Brekka in his European clothes; in long trousers and jacket, with a late Byronesque cravat around his neck.

Likewise the scent raises Hálfdán's spirits, causing him to forget his sorrow.

"Wh-what's that c-called?"

"Tea."

Fridrik pours the tea into the cups and slips the cozy over the English china pot. Hálfdán takes his cup in both hands, raises it to his lips and sips the drink.

"Tea?"

It's strange that so good a drop should have such a small name. It should have been called Illustreret Tidende, that's the grandest name the eejit knows:

"I-is it Danish?"

"No, it's from the mountain Himalaya, which is so high that if you climbed our mountain thirteen times, you still wouldn't have reached the top. Halfway up the slopes of the great mountain is the parish of Darjeeling. And when the birds in Darjeeling break into their dawn chorus, life quickens on the paths that link the tea gardens to the villages: it's the tea pickers going to their work; they may be poorly dressed, yet some have silver rings in their noses."

"I-is it thrushes singing?" asks the eejit.

"No, it's the song sparrow, and under its clear song you can hear the tapping of a woodpecker."

"N-no birds I know?"

"I expect there are wagtails," answers Fridrik.

Hálfdán nods and sips his tea. Meanwhile Fridrik twists up his mustache on the left-hand side and continues his tale:

"At the garden gate they each take their basket and the day's work begins. From then until suppertime the harvesters will pick the topmost leaves from every plant, and their fingertips will be the tea's first staging post on the long journey that may end, for example, in the teapot here at Brekka."

So this morning hour passes.

It is daylight when Fridrik and the eejit Hálfdán come out of the farmhouse with the coffin between them. They carry it easily; the dead woman was not large and the coffin is no work of art, knocked together from scraps of timber found around the farm—but it'll do and seems sound enough. The mare Rosa waits out in the yard, sated with hay. The men place the coffin on a sled, lash it down good and hard, and fasten it either side of the saddle with long spars, which lie along the horse's flanks and are tied firmly to the sled.

After this is done, Fridrik takes an envelope from his jacket. He shows it to Hálfdán and says:

"You're to give Reverend Baldur this letter as soon as the funeral is over. If he asks for it before, tell him I forgot to give it to you. Then you're to remember it when he has finished the ceremony."

He pushes the envelope deep into the eejit's pocket, patting the pocket firmly:

"When the funeral's over . . ."

And they say goodbye, the man who owned Abba and her sweetheart—former sweetheart.

•

Brekka in the Dale, January 8, 1883
Dear Archdeacon Baldur Skuggason,

I enclose the sum of thirty-four crowns. It is payment for the funeral of the woman Hafdís Jónsdóttir, and is to cover wages for yourself and six pallbearers, carriage of the coffin from the farm to the church, lying in state, three knells, and payment for coffee, sugar, and bread for yourself and the pallbearers, as well as any mourners who may attend.

I do not insist on any singing over the woman, nor any address or recital of ancestry. You are to be guided by your own taste and inclinations, or those of any congregation.

I have seen to the coffin and shroud myself, being familiar with the task from my student days in Copenhagen, as your brother Valdimar can attest.

I hope this now completes our business with regard to Hafdís Jónsdóttir's funeral service.

Your obedient servant,
Fridrik B. Fridjónsson

PS Last night I dreamed of a blue vixen. She ran along the screes, heading up the valley. She was as fat as butter, with a pelt of prodigious thickness.

F. B. F.

•

Now the foolish funeral procession lacks for nothing. It sets out from the yard, that is to say, it slides headlong down the slopes, until man, horse, and corpse recover their equilibrium on the riverbank. One could skate along it up the valley, all the way to the church doors at Botn.

Herb-Fridrik goes into the house. He hopes that Hálfdán, eejit that he is, won't break open the coffin and peep inside on the way.

On Saturday, April 18, 1868, a great cargo ship ran aground at Onglabrjotsnef on the Reykjanes peninsula, a black-tarred triple-master with three decks. The third mast had been chopped down, by which means the crew had saved themselves, and the ship was left unmanned, or so it was thought. The splendor of everything aboard this gigantic vessel was such an eye-opener that no one who hadn't seen it for himself would have believed it.

The cabin on the top deck was so large that it could have housed an entire village. It was clear that the cabin had originally been highly decorated, but the gilding and paint had worn off, and all was now squalid inside. Once, it had been divided up into smaller compartments, but now the bulkheads had been removed and sordid pallets lay scattered hither and thither; it would have resembled a ghost ship, had it not been for the stench of urine. There were no sails, and the remaining tatters and cables were all rotten.

The bowsprit was broken and the figurehead degraded; it had been the image of a queen, but her face and breasts had been hacked away with the sharp point of a knife: clearly the ship had once, long ago, been the pride of her captain, but had later fallen into the hands of unscrupulous rogues.

It was hard to guess how long the ship had been at sea or when she had met with her fate. There were no logbooks and her name was almost entirely obliterated from bow and stern; though in one place the lettering ". . . Der Deck . . ." was visible and in another "V . . . r . . . ec . . ."—so people guessed she was Dutch in origin.

When this titanic ship ran aground the surf was too rough for putting to sea; any attempt at salvage or rescue was unthinkable. But when an opportunity finally arose, the men of Sudurnes flocked on board and set to in earnest. They broke up the top deck and discovered, to general rejoicing, that the ship was loaded entirely with fish-liver oil. It was stored in barrels of uniform size, stacked in rows, which were so well lashed down that they had to send out to seven parishes for crowbars to free them. This served well.

After three weeks' work the men had unloaded the cargo from the upper deck onto shore; it amounted to nine hundred barrels of fish-liver oil.

Experiments with the oil proved that it was excellent lighting fuel, but it resembled nothing the people knew, either in smell or taste; though perhaps a faint hint of singed human hair accompanied the burning. Malicious tongues in other parts of the country might claim that the oil was plainly "human suet," but they could keep their slander and envy—nothing detracted from the joy of the folk in the southwest over this windfall that the Almighty Lord had brought to their shore so unlooked for, and involving so little effort, loss of life, or expense to themselves.

They now broke open the middle deck, which contained no fewer barrels of oil than the upper; and although the unloading was carried out with manly zeal, they seemed to make no impression. Then, one day, they became aware of life on board. Something moved in the dark corner by the stern, on the port side, accessible by a gangway running between the hull and the triple rows of barrels. There came a sound of sighing and moaning, accompanied by a metallic clanking.

These were uncanny sounds and men were filled with misgiving. Three stout fellows volunteered to enter the gloom and see what they should see. But just as they were preparing to pounce on the unlooked-for danger, a pathetic creature crept out from under the stack of barrels, and the men very nearly stabbed and crushed it to death with their crowbars, so great was their shock at the sight.

It was an adolescent girl. Her dark hair fell like a

wild growth from her head, her skin was swollen and sore with filth; her nakedness was covered by nothing but a torn, stinking sack. There was an iron manacle around her left ankle, which chained her to one of the great ship's timbers, and from her miserable couch it was not hard to guess what use the crew had made of her. Then there was a bundle that she held in a viselike grip and would not be parted from.

"Abba . . ." she said, so emptily that they shuddered, but she could give no further account of herself, despite being questioned. The salvage men realized that she was a simpleton, and some thought she looked as if she was carrying. They brought the girl and bundle ashore and delivered them into the hands of the sheriff's wife. There she was given food and allowed to sleep two nights in a bed before being dressed in fresh clothes and sent to Reykjavík.

The salvage team was still busy on the third Sunday in June, when the mail ship *Arkturux* rounded the cape of Reykjanes. As she passed the wreck of the oil ship, the passengers gathered at the rail to gaze at the colossus that lay stranded in the bay.

The oil porters took a break from their work and waved to the passengers, who waved back blearily, newly emerged from three days' filthy weather north of the Faroes.

Among the passengers was a tall young man. He had a brown-checked woolen blanket around his shoulders, a gray bowler hat on his head, and a long-stemmed pipe in his mouth.

He was Fridrik B. Fridjónsson.

Herb-Fridrik fills his pipe and contemplates the bundle that sits on the parlor table where the coffin had rested an hour before. It is wrapped in black canvas and tied up with three-ply string—which has held up well despite not having been touched for over seventeen years—and measures some sixteen inches high, twelve inches long, and exactly ten wide. Fridrik grasps the bundle firmly, raises it to head height, and shakes it against his ear. The contents are fixed, weight around ten pounds, nothing rattles inside. Any more than it ever has.

Fridrik puts it back on the table and goes into the kitchen. He pokes a match into the stove and carries the flame to his pipe, lighting it with slow, deliberate sucks. The tobacco crackles, he draws the first smoke of the day deep into his lungs and announces to thin air as he exhales:

"Umph belong Abba."

"Umph" could mean so many things in Abba language: box, chest, casket, ark, or trunk, for example.

Fridrik has long had his suspicions as to what the bundle contains—he has often handled it—but only today will his curiosity be satisfied.

•

Fridrik crossed paths with Hafdís three days after his arrival in Iceland. He was on his way home from a dinner engagement, a gargantuan coffee-drinking session and singsong at the home of his former tutor, Mr. G—. He let his legs decide the route. They swiftly bore him up from Kvosin, out of town, south over the stony ground and down to the sea, where he ran along the ocean shore, yelling to bright infinity:

"I pay homage to you, ocean, O mirror of the free man!"

It was Midsummer's Eve, flies were swinging on the stalks, a ringed plover piped, and the rays of the midnight sun barred the grass.

In those days the capital was small enough that a sound-limbed man could walk around it in half an hour, so Fridrik was soon back where his evening stroll had started—on the track behind the house of the old, gray tutor, Mr. G—. The cook's son came out of the back door, taking care not to drop a tray bearing a tin cup, potato peelings, trout skin, and a hunk of bread; leftovers from the feast earlier in the evening.

Fridrik paused when he saw the boy take this to a

tumbledown shed, which leaned up against another slightly larger outhouse in the backyard. There the boy opened a hatch and eased the tray inside. From the lean-to came a scrambling and snorting, a clatter and grunting. The boy snatched back his hand, slammed the hatch, and hurried away, bumping straight into Fridrik, who had entered through the gate.

"What have you got there, a Danish merchant?"

He said this in a mock-serious tone to soften its severity. The youth gaped at Fridrik as if he were one of Baron Munchhausen's moon men, then answered grumpily:

"Oh, I reckon it's that hussy what did away with her child last week."

"You don't say?"

"Yes, the one what was taken in the graveyard, burying the child's corpse in Olafur 'student' Jónsson's grave."

"And why is she here?"

"I 'spect the bailiff asked his cousin to hold her. They hardly dare put her in the jail with the men, says Mother."

"And what's to be done with her?"

"Oh, I 'spect she'll be sent to Copenhagen for punishment, and sold to the lowest bidder when she comes back. If she comes back."

The lad darted a shifty glance around and pulled a small snuff horn from his pocket.

"Anyhow, I'm not s'posed to talk about what I hear in the house . . ."

He raised the horn to one nostril and sniffed with all his might. With that the conversation was at an end. While the cook's son struggled with his sneeze, Fridrik went over to the lean-to. Squatting down, he pulled the cover from the hatch and peered inside. It was dim but the summer night cast enough blue light through the roof slats for his eyes to grow accustomed to the gloom, and he made out the figure of a woman in one corner. It was the prisoner.

She sat on the earthen floor with her legs straight out in front of her, hunched over the tray like a rag doll. In one small hand she held a strip of potato peel that she was using to push together fish-skin and bread, which she then pinched, raised to her mouth, and chewed conscientiously. She took a sip from the tin cup and heaved a sigh. At that point Fridrik felt he had seen more than enough of the unhappy creature. He fumbled for the cover to close the hatch, bumping his hand on the wall with a loud knock. The figure in the corner became aware of him. She looked up and met his eyes; she smiled and her smile doubled the happiness of the world.

But before he could nod in return, the smile vanished from her face and was at once replaced by a mask so tragic that Fridrik burst into tears.

•

Fridrik unties the knot, winds the string around the fingers of his left hand, slides the coil over his fingertips, and slips it into his waistcoat pocket. He unwraps the canvas from the bundle. Two packages of equal size come to light, wrapped in waxed brown paper. He lays them side by side and opens them. The contents of each appear to be the same: black wooden tablets, twenty-four in each pile. He turns over the tablets like cards from a pack, and notes that they are painted black on one side, white on the other; not all of them, however, because in one pile some of the tablets are black and green, while in the other they are black and blue. He scratches his beard.

"Well, Abba-di, it's quite something, this picture puzzle that you've carried through life . . ."

And now a strange and intricate spectacle unfolds in the little parlor at Brekka in the Dale. The master of the house handles each piece of the puzzle with care, examining it from every angle; the green and blue faces have lettering on them—a sentence in Latin—which simplifies the game.

He begins the jigsaw.

Starting with the blue tablets.

Fridrik B. Fridjónsson studied natural history at the University of Copenhagen from 1862 to 1865. Like so many of his countrymen, he did not finish his degree, and for his last three years in Denmark he was a regular employee of the Elefant Pharmacy, then under the management of the pharmacist Ørnstrup, in Store Kongensgade. There Fridrik worked his way up to the position of medical assistant, helping with the pharmacist's catalogue of inebriants: ether, opium, laughing gas, fly agaric, belladonna, chloroform, mandragora, hashish, and coca. In addition to being used for various cures, these substances were greatly favored by the lotus-eaters of Copenhagen.

The lotus-eaters were a group who modeled their way of life on the poetry of French writers such as Baudelaire, de Nerval, Gautier, and de Musset. They threw parties—which gave birth to many rumors, but few attended—at which narcotic plants bore away the guests swiftly and sweetly to new worlds, both in flesh and in spirit. Fridrik was a frequent guest at these gatherings, and once, when they stood up from their ether-driven roller coasters, he announced to his traveling companions:

"I have seen the universe! It is made of poems!"

"Spoken like *en rigtig Islænding*, a true Icelander," said the Danes.

Fridrik's trip to Iceland in the summer of 1868 was, on the other hand, a far more earthbound affair. He had come to sell up his parents' farm following their deaths from pneumonia, nine days apart, that spring. There were no assets to speak of: the remote croft of Brekka, the cow Crooked Horn, a few scrawny ewes, a fiddle, a chessboard, a bookcase, his mother's spinning wheel, and the tomcat Little Frikki. So the plan was to make his stay brief; it wouldn't take long to sell the livestock to the neighbors, pay off the debts, pack up the furnishings, hang the cat, and burn the farm buildings, which were crumbling into the hillside, to the best of Fridrik's knowledge.

And this is what he would have done if the universe had not thrown up an unexpected riddle in a filthy outhouse one sunny night in June.

•

The wooden tablets play in Fridrik's hands; what had looked like an incomprehensible puzzle now guides his fingers. It's as if the riddle is solving itself by magic;

without conscious intent the man lays one tablet against another and the moment their edges touch, one slides into the other's groove and then will not be budged; and so on and on, until the blue tablets have formed a base, while the others are the walls and gable ends of what resembles a long, quite deep trough; white-walled within, black without.

And the sentence on the base resolves itself: *Omnia mutantur—nihil interit*. Fridrik laughs scornfully: "All things change—nothing perishes." He can't imagine what cunning craftsman could have given Hafdís this object, choosing for her a quotation from Ovid, no less.

There is a lowing from the back of the house.

The riddle solver wakes from his thoughts; Crooked Horn the Second is demanding attention. Fridrik puts down the creation and hurries to the barn; he hasn't yet got the hang of the new household arrangements at Brekka; the animals used to be Abba's concern.

•

Twenty-riksdaler stipends went to students at the university who were encumbered with the task of accompanying friendless folk to the grave. Fridrik performed this dreary duty like anyone else, but as he was a hopeless bibliomaniac and forever in the red with Høst the bookseller, he welcomed the chance to take the night watch at the city mortuary. While there he took on yet another job—that of translating articles from foreign medical journals for a thick-witted but well-to-do pathological anatomy student from Christiania.

Fridrik sat many a night by a smoking lamp, translating into Danish descriptions of the latest methods of keeping us poor humans alive, while on pallets around him lay the corpses, beyond any aid, despite the encouraging news of advances in electrical cures.

In the third volume of *London Hospital Reports, 1866*, Fridrik read an article on the classification of idiots by J. Langdon H. Down, a London doctor. The article was an attempt to explain a phenomenon that had long puzzled people: the fact that white women sometimes gave birth to defective children of Asiatic stock. The doctor conjectured that the mother's illness or a shock during pregnancy might have caused the child to be born prematurely. This could happen anywhere in the well-documented developmental stages of the fetus: fish–lizard–bird–dog–ape–Negro–yellow man–Indian–white man, but seemed most common at the seventh stage.

Down's Mongoloid children had therefore not attained full development; they were doomed to be childish and meek all their lives. But like other members of inferior races, with kind treatment and patience they could be taught many useful skills.

In Iceland they were destroyed at birth.

Unlike other types of cretins, where it cannot be seen

until too late that they do not have their full wits, no one could fail to see that a Down's child was made according to a different recipe from the rest of us, even of different, alien ingredients: it had coarser hair, a yellowish complexion, stumpy body, flabby skin, and eyes slanted like slits in a canvas.

No witnesses were needed; before the child could utter its first wail, the midwife would close its nose and mouth, thereby returning its breath to the great cauldron of souls from which all mankind is served.

The child was said to have been stillborn and its body was consigned to the nearest priest. He confirmed its nature, buried the poor creature, and that was the end of the story.

But there were always some such unfortunate infants that managed to survive. It happened in godforsaken out-of-the-way places where there was no one to talk sense into the mothers, who thought they could cope with the children, odd though they were. Then of course they got lost, wandering off in their ignorance, leaving their bones on mountain paths, turning up half-dead in the summer pastures, or simply stumbling into the lives of strangers.

And as the poor wretches didn't know who they were or where they had blown in from, the authorities would settle them on whichever farm they happened to have ended up at.

The farmers were greatly annoyed by these "gifts from heaven," and the household found it degrading to have to share sleeping quarters with a defective.

·

There was no question that the unfortunate girl imprisoned in the bailiff of Reykjavík's kinsman's backyard was one of those Asiatic innocents who owned nothing but the breath in her lungs.

Wiping the food off her hands, she embraced the young man's head as he wept in the chicken hatch, comforting him with the following words:

"Furru amh-amh, furru amh-amh . . ."

Twilight deepens in the valley; the afternoon night begins its journey up the slopes. The darkness seems to flow from the open grave in the western corner of the churchyard at Botn, as if the shadow grows there first, before darkening the whole world. It's a near thing with the light: four men appear in the church doorway with a coffin on their shoulders, the parson hard on their heels, followed by several of those black-clad crones who are never ill when there's someone to be seen to the grave. The funeral cortege proceeds rapidly, as if in a dance, their short steps breaking into quick variations, for the churchyard path is as slippery as glass, although Hálfdán Atlason had been sent to break up the surface while they sang over his lady friend in church. Now he stands by the lych-gate, tolling the funeral bell.

A gust carries the copper song down the valley into Fridrik's parlor, where he hears its echo—no, it's the knowledge that Abba's funeral is taking place at this moment that has rung the tiniest bell in his mind.

He's putting the finishing touches on the puzzle's companion piece; it's the exact image of the other, except that its base is green, with a different Latin tag. This is also by the author of *Metamorphoses*, translating as: "The burden that is well borne becomes light."

The moment Reverend Baldur's pallbearers lower the coffin into the black grave at Botn, it not only becomes pitch black in the valley but light is shed on the contents of the parcel that Hafdís Jónsdóttir brought with her north to the Dale, when Fridrik B. Fridjónsson, favorite student of a close kinsman of the bailiff, got her absolved from the charge of exposing her child, on the grounds of ignorance, and on condition that she would remain in his care for as long as she lived.

Yes, if the two halves of the puzzle were laid together they would form an artfully crafted, highly polished coffin.

•

When Fridrik B. Fridjónsson rode north with his peculiar maidservant and settled on his father's estate at Brekka, the parish of Dale was served by a burned-out priest popularly known as "Reverend Jakob with the pupil" Hallsson, who as a child had taken out one of his eyes with a fishhook.

This incompetent minister was so used to his parishioners' boorishness—scuffles, belches, farts, and heckling—that he affected not to hear when Abba chimed in during his altar service, which she did both loud and clear and never in tune. He was more worried that the precentor would drown in his neighbors' spittle. This fellow, a farmer by the name of Gilli Sigurgillason from Barnahamrar, possessed a powerful voice and sang in fits and starts, gaping so wide at the high notes that you could see right down his gullet, and the congregation used to amuse themselves by lobbing wet plugs of tobacco into his mouth—many of them had become quite good shots.

Four years later Reverend Jakob died, greatly regretted by his flock; he was remembered as ugly and tedious, but good with children.

His successor was Reverend Baldur Skuggason, who introduced a new era in church manners to the Dale. Men sat quietly on the benches, holding their tongues while the parson preached the sermon, having learned how he dealt with rowdies: he summoned them to meet him after the service, took them around the back of the church, and beat the living daylights out of them. The women, meanwhile, turned holy from the first day and behaved as if they had never taken part in teasing "the Reverend with the pupil." They said it served the louts to whom they were married or betrothed right, they should have been thrashed long ago; for the new parson was a childless widower.

Gilli from Barnahamrar now sang louder than ever, at the speed of a piston, with mouth gaping wide. But Fridrik was asked to leave Abba at home: the word of God must reach the ears of the congregation "uninterrupted by the ravings of an idiot," as Reverend Baldur put it after the first and only time Abba attended one of his services.

There was no shifting him from this position; he would not have her anywhere near him. And none of the newly civilized and well-thrashed parishioners would speak up for a simple woman who knew no greater happiness than to dress up in her Sunday best and attend church with other people.

After this, Fridrik and Hafdís had few dealings with the folk of the Dale. Hálfdán Atlason sneaked a visit to Abba when he could. But the parson of Botn took a wide detour when he met them on the road.

·

The churchyard at Botn stands on the banks of the Botnsa River. This is a middling-size, smooth stream, of a good depth and high-banked, bordered by spongy patches of marsh, with plenty of good peat land and enough of that deceptive surface rust. After a winter of heavy snow the river runs wild, bursting its banks with such demonic force that the dirty gray meltwater surges out of its course, flooding the marshes and forming lakes in the graveyard, leaving the church stranded on an island in its midst. The water-ringed house of God remains cut off until the graveyard has swallowed enough of the mountain milk for the water to just cover a maiden's ankle; by then the sanctified ground is drunk and wobbles underfoot until well into summer.

After such fits in the Botnsa, the riverbank gives way and the churchyard crumbles into the river. Then it is clear that nature has treated the dead with so little respect that all is reduced to a mush: teeth and coccyx, fingers and toes, adults and children, lower jawbones and scalps, buttocks here, a woman's pelvis there, a vertebra from this century, a man's paunch from the last but one.

No, one couldn't exactly say that "the Lord's garden" here in the Dale was cultivated; and men had to be true neighbors to be willing to revisit their neighbors in this condition.

So it was that on Monday, January 8, 1883, Reverend Baldur performed the funeral rites on the company that Herb-Fridrik considered worthy of those who could not bring themselves to allow a simpleton to sing out of key with her parish priest: a quilt cover stuffed with sixty-six pounds of cow dung, the skeleton of a decrepit ewe, an empty aquavit cask, some rotten barrel staves, and a moldy urine tub.

Abba deserved a different soul mate, fairer earth.

Ghost-sun is a name given by poets to their friend the moon, and it is fitting tonight when its ashen light bathes the grove of trees that stand in the dip above the farmhouse at Brekka. This little copse was the loving creation of Abba and Fridrik, and few things made them more of a laughingstock in the Dale than its cultivation, though most of their endeavors met with ridicule.

The rowan draws shadow pictures on the snow crust; there's a low sough in the naked boughs and the odd twig still bears a cluster of dried berries that the birds over-looked last year.

Fridrik toils slowly up the slope; he has a woman's body in his arms. In the middle of the grove is a freshly dug grave; on the edge of the grave stands an open coffin. The man approaches the coffin and lays the body inside. Then he hurries back, but the moon remains.

Hafdís is well equipped for her final journey. She's dressed in her Sunday best and great care has been taken with every aspect of her costume: on her head sits a cap with a long tassel and an oft-twisted silver tube; around her neck is a violet silk scarf; her jacket is of English cloth and the embroidered borders of her bodice are visible beneath; her apron is sewn from rose damask and the buttons, cast in white silver, bear an elaborate "A"; her skirt is striped with cross-stitched velvet bands and her legs are encased in red socks and high black stockings; her shoes are of heather-colored calfskin with white stitching; and on her hands she wears black mittens, with roses in four colors knitted on the backs.

Abba bought these rich clothes for herself, paying out of the wages she received for assisting with the unusual farming that is practiced at Brekka; on the one hand the collecting of plants, on the other the creation of small books on Icelandic flora: "with fifty-seven genuine dried samples," as was said of them in the article about Iceland in the *Illustrierte Zeitung*. These were the sorts of books romantic young men gave to their future brides, and the last pages were left empty for the composition of pretty poems.

Fridrik kneels beside the coffin, holding a different sort of book; it is thick and psalter-like, with the odd bird's feather sticking out from between the pages. This is Abba's bird book, in which she collected feathers with passion and exactitude. She glued them to the pages, and under her instruction Fridrik recorded the names and gender of the birds, and the provenance of the feathers.

He had often wondered where Abba had picked up all her bird lore, but there were no answers to be had from her, and when he tried to teach her more natural history, she thanked him politely, saying merely that she was interested in birds.

On the title page she herself had written: "BiRRds of tHE WOrld—AbbA fRom BreKKa."

Fridrik places the book on Abba's breast and lays her hands to rest in a cross on top. He inadvertently holds them tighter than intended and feels the small fingers through the mittens. This cheers him a little; these are the hands that comforted him after he lost his parents.

He kisses her brow.

He closes the coffin.

Fridrik finishes filling in the grave. He takes off his woolen cap, folds it, and puts it in his jacket pocket. He pulls off his gloves and shoves them in his armpits.

He falls to his knees.

He bows his head.

He sighs sorrowfully.

Straightening up, he gazes down through the earth to where he pictures Abba's face, and recites two verses for her. The first is an optimistic poem; a little bird rhyme of his own making:

> A summer bird sang
> On a sunny day:
> Happiness led me,
> O'er the airy way
> My friend for to see.
> The little bird sang
> Of its rowan tree.

The second is the introduction to a lost ballad. It tells of the equality that all living beings are ensured in death, without any need for revolution:

> Earth fails,
> All grows old and worn.
> Flesh is dust—however it's adorned.

Rising to his feet, he puts on his cap, reaches into his pocket for a little pipe made from a sheep's leg bone, and plays a tune from "On the Death of a Nightingale" by the late Franz Schubert, thus linking the two poetic fragments.

Then at last Fridrik's eyes fill with tears: they set off down his cheeks but dry up halfway; it's cold out. He bids farewell to Hafdís Jónsdóttir with the same words as she took her leave of him:

"Abba-ibo!"

•

Between the peaks to the west, there is a glimpse of the universe where three stars of the constellation Cygnus glitter.

Heavy banks of cloud overshadow the valley.

It snows until late in the morning.

The sky is clear and the first blush of day at its winter blackest. Fridrik B. Fridjónsson stands out in the yard at Brekka, hidden by the farmhouse door, smoking opium-moistened tobacco in his pipe.

Something brushes against his foot: the oldest tom-cat in northern Europe: Little Frikki. He's cold after his feline "Winterreise" and wants to be let in. His namesake obliges him.

Shortly afterward he sees a man emerge from the farmhouse at Dalbotn. It's Reverend Baldur Skuggason, like a little bump in the landscape. A tiny stick juts up from his left shoulder: his gun.

He slides down over the home fields, then sets a course north over the Asar for the cliffs at Bjarg.

Herb-Fridrik knocks out his pipe on the heel of his shoe.

And goes inside to sleep.

III

(JANUARY 11–17, 1883)

The shot fires off. It blows away the divine peace of the wilderness like a scrap of paper. A shower of sparks bursts from the barrel. The gunpowder crack shouts: "HEAR THE MAN!"

The vixen is thrown up in the air with a pathetic whine.

Reverend Baldur crawls to his feet.

Purple suns and streaks of lightning dazzle his eyes, there's a harsh jangling in his ears. His legs are stiff from lying in the snow but the lifeblood surges through his body as soon as he moves.

The priest creeps over to the rock and checks on the little fox. Yes, there she lies, dead as a doornail. He sinks down on his right knee and seizes the fur by the tail; it appears quite intact—there'll be some value in that.

He straightens up, cramming the vixen inside his coat.

•

The highest knob of the Asheimar peak is known as the eastern high knob. The peak faces more or less west, but has a razor-sharp horn, which means that the slope known as the southern slope in fact faces south-southwest.

In northeasterly blizzards a vast snowdrift forms on the south face of this horn, stretching right from the highest pinnacle down to the roots of the peak.

There stood Reverend Baldur, the firearm in his left hand, his right arm buried up to the wrist in his coat, like Napoleon in the desert.

When the peak replied to his shot.

·

The drift splits in the middle with such a thunderous crack that the loose snow is whirled up around Reverend Baldur, obscuring his figure and blotting out his view in all directions. The lower section of the drift sets off down the mountain—snatching up the priest on the way.

He somersaulted over the precipice, landing alternately on hands and feet, tumbling over and over, losing both his fur hat and his gun. He was carried for a long way on all fours before finally landing on both feet at once. Then he managed to withstand the avalanche for a brief moment before it knocked him flat—and after that he was carried along alternately over or under the snow; sometimes half, mostly wholly submerged. In this way Reverend Baldur took flight.

All the time he remained perfectly conscious, never buried for long.

·

The man traveled some two hundred yards downhill in this manner before the avalanche came to a halt. This was by the high crags on the brink of Freyja's Chair, as they call the deep bowl in the slopes of Asheimar. Below that lies the steep slope of the Kinnar, light of brow, beneath the foot of the glacier.

Reverend Baldur lay still, recovering from his journey. He was winded and coughed a little, having scarcely drawn breath during his descent. He couldn't expand his chest for the weight of snow pressing on every side. He was completely buried, apart from his head and right shoulder, which protruded from the snow. He tried to move but could barely twitch his right foot or shrug his shoulder. There was a pain in his left thigh and he suspected it was broken, as his leg was numb.

The weather was mild, with light cloud and a gentle southerly breeze; the winter sun floated over the wilderness, fat and red as the yolk of a raven's egg. This was the calm that had ridden on the wings of yesterday's storm.

•

A shadow darkened the snow crust and a moment later a raven landed there. It cocked its head on one side, examining the man stuck fast in the snow trap. Reverend Baldur jerked his head and shooed the unwelcome visitor away:

"Damn you, you ugly cur of Odin!"

But the raven was no more obedient than usual. It called to its namesake and the next time the priest looked around there were two of them. They waddled to and fro, sharpening their beaks, occasionally craning their necks toward the man and breaking out in a hideous carrion song:

"Kark, kark . . ."

They took little hops toward him, like eager guests at a feast. But when the larger raven snatched at the priest's scarf and began to tear out the wool, Reverend Baldur felt it was high time he put an end to this provocation. After a great argument with the drift he managed to wrangle his right leg free, and shortly afterward it yielded up his arm.

Finally, after a long and weary struggle, he crawled out of the "snow-white tomb," having spent most of his time keeping the ravens at bay with snowballs and threats.

•

Although Reverend Baldur was now aboveground, he wasn't quite free of the snow. It had drifted into his clothes during his breakneck descent and lay between the layers, even against his bare skin. And now the slush began to run down his body in icy streams, from his armpits, down his chest and back, and into his shoes.

The priest growled low as the water turned tepid on his battered body.

•

Reverend Baldur began to think about his journey home; it looked as if he would have to follow the belt of rock west, all the way to the crevasse . . . Or go in completely the opposite direction and try walking along the Mjadara River . . . Or . . . The priest couldn't complete his thoughts for the ravenous cries of the ravens. They roved around, bent double with hunger, rolled on their backs, croaked, and beat their wings on the frozen earth.

He shook his fist at the birds and yelled:

"Silence, or I'll scorch off your damned heads!"

The household at Dalbotn was familiar with the headache cure of burning a raven's head in a pot and blending strong lye with the ash. The mixture was then smeared on the sore spot and left there until the pain subsided.

And now, as chance would have it, the raven pair obeyed. They fell silent as one, lifted off from the snowfield, and soared easily over the edge of the bowl without so much as flapping a wing. There the updraft caught them and raised them high into the blue.

Then they were beautiful.

•

Reverend Baldur hawked vigorously, intending to spit after the birds, but before he could let fly he heard a deep whistling sound from above. He looked over his shoulder and scanned the peak of Asheimar; the upper part of the drift had vanished from the highest knob.

In that very instant the avalanche paid the priest a visit. It clapped him on the back and swept him over the cliff. On the way he scraped against the edge, flaying his balaclava up to his crown and tearing a chunk of fat from his neck.

During the fall it occurred to him that there was less risk of injury if his body was limp. When he came down on the slope of the Kinnar, he halted for a split second, then was whirled away again twice as fast as before—now headfirst. Reverend Baldur suspected that this was his last hour but took it for granted that he should resist his fate. So he tried to raise his head above the avalanche, lifting it as best he could.

The priest felt as if he were caught in the midst of a raging storm but there were no further discomforts until he began to have difficulty breathing.

•

Shortly afterward the priest's hell ride down the hard-packed snow came to an end.

What happened was that the avalanche reared up like a wave on a stony shore and when it broke on the glacial moraine it shot the man into a small cave—a kind of elongated hollow that had formed at the end of the last ice age when the glacial tongue lumbered over the mountain root, extracting a thirty-yard-long molar of rock.

That is to say, Reverend Baldur came to rest in a hollow under the glacier.

And the avalanche closed it off with its full weight.

He lay on his back, his right leg straight and about a yard higher than his head, his left leg bent and his left arm on his belly. His right arm was also bent and oddly twisted. The haversack had come off his left arm and the leather strap lay about his right elbow, trapping his upper arm.

The priest was not in a good way but this did not bother him, as he was dead to the world.

·

Now it was fortunate for Reverend Baldur that he was well wrapped up.

His mother, Nal Valdimarsdóttir, had dressed him for the fox hunt. He wore thick, homespun undergarments, so well fulled that they could stand up on their own; a middle shirt of rabbit skin; two woolen sweaters, one light and the other very thick; Danish trousers; three pairs of knitted stockings; and unshaven sealskin shoes on his feet. Over all he wore leather trousers and a leather coat; double-breasted with whalebone buttons.

But, most important of all, Nal had equipped her son with a scarf of her own knitting. He had wound the scarf around his head to make himself invisible to the vixen, and this getup had prevented the priest from losing anything in the first avalanche but the hat that perched on top, a German piece made of kid, while on the second journey the scarf had held the balaclava in place, although it was now half off his head.

On his chest he had the wretched vixen.

•

The rock splits open behind the man. In the doorway stands a young woman clad in nothing but blue knitted drawers and a red tasseled cap. She takes the man's hand and guides him into a low-ceilinged chamber. There is a well in the middle of the floor with lead shot floating on the water, not sinking, so the surface is gray with shot.

She points at it and says:

"This is the Well of Life."

The priest stirred.

The glacier admitted a dim blue shadow into the little rock chamber and by that faint light Reverend Baldur could make out his surroundings. He lay at the foot of a wall, which must be the eastern wall. He had scrabbled a little with his left foot in his sleep, but the right leg was still stuck fast, pointing straight up in the air. He couldn't sit up or twist around or free himself, however furiously he struggled.

He soon grew weary from his exertions, a drowsiness fell on him, and he lost consciousness once more.

•

The man thought he must have nodded off, for when he was startled awake by his right leg falling to the floor with a noisy splash, it seemed to him that the very rainbow itself was shining in through the ice eye of the cave mouth. He simply couldn't work out where the colors were coming from, but guessed that it was night outside and the Aurora Borealis sisters had followed him from Asheimar—they were greeting their old friend Baldur Skuggason.

The priest thought this was most obliging of them.

He was feeling rather chilly so he tried to move and that warmed him up again. He drifted off for an hour or so at intervals during the night, shifting position in between times—but not enough to tire himself out. The strap on his haversack grew steadily tighter on his right arm but he couldn't reach the knife in his belt to cut it.

The man knew that it was possible to survive for a

long time in a snowdrift, but expected the glacier to prove a cold bedspread—the advantage was that he would gradually grow wetter from the snow, which was melting around him.

The evening of the second day drew on.

•

Next morning the heat from Reverend Baldur's bodily engine had told upon the snow by his left arm and head. He was reasonably compos mentis and able to rise up on his elbow. He noticed that the snow was dark where his head had dented it. And at this sight he became aware of a stinging in his neck. He pulled off his mitten, reached a hand behind him, and groped his nape: he seemed to have acquired a new mouth where the flesh bulged between neck bone and shirt collar.

He fumbled this phenomenon for a good while before drawing back his hand. It was covered in blood, which appeared black in the deceptive light of the fissure. Reverend Baldur licked the gore from his fingers; nothing nutritious must go to waste. Then he placed the mitten on the wound and bound the scarf around his neck, pulling it good and tight.

He fell into a deep sleep.

•

Twilight fell, not gradually but abruptly, bringing a black murk.

Around midnight, in all likelihood, he sensed a wetness from the snow, and toward morning on the fourth day there had been such a thaw around Reverend Baldur that he was able to remove his belt, get at his knife, and cut through the offending strap. Sitting up, he dragged the haversack to him. There he had provisions: a dried cod's head.

Dried cod's head is not merely food fit for a gentleman; it is also a diversion. As he flayed the flesh from the head, putting it in his mouth on the point of his knife and chewing as slowly as he could, to make it last, the man amused himself by naming all the bones and parts of the head:

"Jawbone, that's the jaw muscle, shoulder bone, that's the shoulder muscle, pillow bone, that's the pillow muscle, raven bone, that's the raven muscle, gum, that's the gum muscle, cheek, that's the cheek muscle, nape, that's the nape muscle, bell, that's the bell muscle.

"And that's all the bones in this old head!"

Reverend Baldur burst out laughing. He pictured that ancient hag, his mother, with the hook bone on her shriveled lower lip, mumbling:

"My little bit, my little bit . . ."

The priest couldn't control his mirth. He gripped

his belly and laughed. He laughed until he howled with laughter. He howled with laughter until he cried. He cried and his tears were sore.

Yes, he wept sorely for the evil fate that had left him alone, with no one to share the entertainment that is to be had from a dried cod's head.

•

On the fifth day the priest under the glacier began to fear for his sanity, so he did what comes most naturally to an Icelander when he is in a fix. That is to recite ballads, verses, and rhymes, sing loud and clear to himself and, when all else fails, to recall his hymns. This is a failsafe old trick, if men wish to preserve their wits.

Reverend Baldur embarked conscientiously on his program. He sang and recited all he knew, even the psalms of David. But he had nothing left but Reverend Jochumsson's "big bang" and a comic verse by his colleague Thorarensen, which he meant to leave out and instead start all over again, when he discovered to his amazement that everything that had dropped from his lips up to this point had been wiped from his memory. Not a single word, not a single letter remained.

He reacted quickly, testing whether this was really the case; he thundered all the verses of Jochumsson's "Song of Praise" to himself—and, would you know it?, once he had finished the rendition he couldn't remember a thing.

Then he came to Reverend Gisli's verses.

·

SHOPPING LIST FOR THE MERCHANT'S

Paper and ink and pens and wax,
raisins and prunes and hemp and flax,
baccy, pepper, and camphor oil,
a hundredweight of coffee, hooks and foil,
anvil, window glass, fencing twine,
ginger and rum and good red wine,
from this my need will be quite plain,
the day I meet old Thorgrimsen.

Now my wife comes after, to wit,
and buys a cask of aquavit,
silk cloth, soap, a whistling kettle,
six plates, a chamber pot of metal,
cards and baubles, a cinnamon roll,
she buys as if for life and soul,
I think that if she had her way,
she'd take the merchant any day.

·

The poem droned c-c-constantly in the m-man's h-head like a fly under glass, with-without his being able to resist it. H-he was b-both h-hot and c-cold, ice-hot and boiling-cold at o-once. He t-tried what he c-could to recall oth-other stohories, oth-other p-poems, but it was all-all lost and forgotten, lohost and for-gotten from his deep-frozen memory, he w-was st-stuck with this on h-his b-b-b-boiling b-brain:

Oh, o-o-oh, h-how sham-shaming to d-die with this ab-absurd shopping list, shohopping list, o-on, on m-my li-hip-lihips, thought the pre-pre-hiest.

He p-pursed to-togehether his m-mouhouth to p-prevent, his, his d-dying wohords fr-from behing, for example: "a hundredweight of coffee." Though ih-it w-was truhue that-that he had no-ho witness to his hour of deheath b-but "Aitch Tee"—the H-holy T-trinity—he didn't ca-hare. And j-just f-for a m-moment, Rever-end Baldur f-felt s-s-sorry for h-hims-self, self.

H-he wh-whispered to-the dark-darkness:

'Thi-his is an ug-ugly h-hole . . .'

He felt instantly better.

He closed his eyes.

And awaited his death.

"Ho! Reverend Baldur! Baldur Skuggason! Ho!"

The calls that carried to the ears of the dying man sounded as if they came from the belly of a whale; the voice was muffled, and distance made it, if anything, even shriller:

"Ho, Reverend Baldur, ho!"

The priest was jolted out of his deathly lethargy:

"Ho! I'm here! Ho!"

He fell instantly silent to listen for a response:

"Ho! Ho! Ho!"

He tore off his balaclava and turned his right ear to the livid ice wall, but heard nothing—he turned the left ear: not a sound.

"Down here! Ho! Down here!"

He shouted and yelled, then pricked his ears, moving with great care so the creaking of his leather clothing would not drown out any noises from outside. Yes! There it was; nearer. A reedy voice was calling:

"Are you there? Ho!"

"HO! HERE! HO!" Reverend Baldur howled with all his life and soul.

•

"Do you want to deafen me?"

Reverend Baldur's heart missed a beat. The inquiry did not come from some searcher outside on the snow-field, no, the impertinent inquiry came from someone inside the fissure with him, and not only inside the fissure with him, but right up against him, or to be more precise, from inside his own clothes.

The priest squawked with terror when the vixen stirred at his breast. He writhed on his wet pallet, tearing at his leather coat with such violence that the whalebone buttons popped off and were lost. (Which was a great pity, as they were fine articles that Haraldur, Reverend Baldur's half-brother, had carved with his own hand and given him as a confirmation gift.)

The vixen sprang forth onto the floor of the cave. She spun in a circle, plumped down on her rump—and began to lick herself like a house cat.

•

Reverend Baldur was quick to recover, a man with a priestly training; the naturalist rose up in him. He watched the beast's behavior with scientific detachment.

She was damn sprightly, considering she had been

out cold for six days and nights. It was ridiculous how she worked away at herself so frantically. She licked the bloodstains from her pelt and bored her muzzle to the roots of her fur, gnawing at herself as if she were delousing for doomsday.

The nature observer shut one eye.

"Look at the creature, faugh!"

He slapped his thigh.

"Hah, a vampire drinking its own blood!"

At that point the vixen spat out the first piece of shot. It pinged against the priest's cheek. He moaned aloud and swore. But the vixen ignored him. She continued to preen herself until she had cleaned from her flesh all that the rifle had delivered to her: bloodstained lead ricocheted around the fissure, and great sparks flew from the rock where the shot struck.

The priest was hard-pressed to avoid the hail of lead that whined around him like a swarm of midges.

•

The vixen now began to pace back and forth, to and fro, here and there. Reverend Baldur sat quietly in his place, with his hands in his lap. He avoided meeting the beast's eyes; it seemed edgy and incalculable.

Time passed.

At first light next day the vixen stopped and said:

"Well, Parson, what do we do now?"

"We could argue," he answered.

"What should we argue about?" she asked.

"Electricity," said the priest.

The vixen regarded him as if he were a fool:

"If you think a wild beast like me knows the first thing about electricity, you're sadly mistaken . . ."

But Reverend Baldur was so insistent, he suggested to the vixen that if she could solve a riddle he knew, she would be allowed to decide the topic of argument; if not, they would argue about electricity. The vixen agreed:

"Out with it, then . . ."

"I'm born with a loud noise, and yet I have no voice."

The vixen took thought—for far too long, in Reverend Baldur's opinion, but he said nothing, he didn't dare alarm her—and in the end she gave in.

"Do you give in?"

The priest laughed at the beast's stupidity: "It's a fart!"

And he broke wind in support of his point.

"How predictable," replied the vixen, drily:

"Go on, then, argue about electricity."

•

By rights the electricity debate should have taken place in a grander setting than the stony crack in a glacier's backside. The fact of the case was that Reverend Baldur had been invited to Reykjavík to talk about this interest of his at a public, advertised meeting. There he meant to oppose some Icelandic-Canadian émigré who was preaching Edison's great tidings to his former countrymen.

If the avalanche had not taken him, the priest would have returned home to Dalbotn the morning after the fox hunt. He would have put the finishing touches on his speech and then reached the capital four days later, at noon on January 15, and that evening he would have wiped both his nose and his arse with his opponent. By his calculations, the meeting must have taken place three days ago; quarreling with the vixen about the matter was some compensation.

So the priest expounded his religious theories for the beast, for against electricity he had theological arguments. These theories were highly modern, because Reverend Baldur believed in a material God, self-created, both visible and tangible—compare: "When it snows on man, it rains on God."

Consequently he could not accept that electricity, which is created by the friction of the smallest atoms of the world, which form the kernel of God, should be transmitted via wires and cables, here, there, and everywhere, even into factories where it would be used to drive machines that, for example, might spit out meatballs, yes, or mustard.

What had she to say to that?

•

The vixen decided to meet the priest on his home ground:

"But if electricity is the building material of the world, and light its revelation, compare the first book of Moses, and God himself is a being of light, though perhaps we can't see this with the naked eye—like the pitch-black rock that surrounds us—well, couldn't you say then that in reality it is one all-embracing world mission to bring God into people's homes via electric power lines; even illuminate whole cities with him—n'est-ce pas?"

She looked inquiringly at the priest. He returned her look in silence; she tweaked the argument:

"Surely the transmission of electric power ought to be desirable in the eyes of the Church, and its servants, if it is the Almighty Himself who shines in the lamps."

He did not reply. Had she stumped him, then? No, the little fox had not noticed that while she was talking, Reverend Baldur had drawn the knife from its sheath and hidden it in his hand; the one facing the rock wall.

Then he said gently:

"Do you really believe, Madam Vixen, that the radiance from these electric bulbs of yours can penetrate the human soul?"

Before she had a chance to answer, the man plunged his knife deep into the vixen's breast.

He raised the vixen's remains on the blade of his knife and stared into her dull eyes; the pupils were filmy like moorland tarns in the first freeze of winter, but all the priest saw was that she was dead at last.

The corpse lay limp in his hands and he discovered that the skin was strangely loose on the body; a sure sign of a witch's familiar—since the night she had tried to drive him mad by dividing herself into four, he had suspected that that is exactly what she was: a witch's familiar. His ruse of luring her into talk had been successful. The sender had been careless, he had put too much of himself into her, spoken unwittingly through her. Yes, the use of French at the end of her speech about the city of lights had given the beast away. The priest was in no doubt as to who had sent him Vixen-Reynard's daughter.

The demon bore every sign of having been raised against him by that fool of a sheriff from Fjord, Valdimar Skuggason, his elder brother. This upstart had never forgiven Reverend Baldur for the fact that in her widowhood their mother, Nal, had chosen to live at the Botn parsonage, taking with her their patrimony, the hymnbook collection of "Old" Skuggi Haraldsson from Saurar.

No, she wasn't put off by the fact that her Baldur

had never left these shores nor that he had received all his education from an Icelandic priest's school.

•

Reverend Baldur Skuggason skinned the vixen, thinking of his brother Valdi with quiet vengeance all the while, cutting along the animal's back, hacking a groove beside the spine, from ruff to tail: yes, he'd get his just desserts; he groped inside the body with his hands, down along the flanks, squeezing his fingers between flesh and hide, leaving the fat behind in the belly: he would bring a charge against him at the high court for attempted murder; he snapped the outer limbs from their sockets, cut a ring around the paws, and forced the legs out of their socks, he jabbed his forefinger into the muzzle, tore the nose from the skull with his nail; he would go to the gallows, the damn mountebank—and so the man tugged and tore and toiled until he had ripped the animal from its blue pelt.

The priest stripped naked. He gouged the fat out of the skin bag and greased himself from top to toe. Then he dressed himself in the hide, which proved so roomy that its forelegs reached the ground. The vixen herself wasn't much to look at where she lay on the stones, naked as a fetus in the womb. The man stuck his finger into her rib cage, plucked out her heart, and laid it on his tongue:

It's like ptarmigan, thought Reverend Baldur, pulling the skin over his head. He swallowed the slimy fox heart, and as if he'd been struck by lightning the thought flashed through him—OUT!

•

Reverend Baldur dug himself out of the avalanche. He used both jaws and claws, he no longer knew his name, he just scratched and gnawed, gnawed and scratched.

The blood throbbed in his temples.

"Light, more light!"

But the closer the priest came to his goal, the less man there was in him, the more beast.

He stands shivering on the glacial moraine, gulping down the refreshing mountain air. The morning sun blesses and restores him.

Below his feet lies a long, quite narrow, green valley. There are fair slopes, grown with grass and willow scrub. A river runs down the middle; a char flashes under the surface, a phalarope floats above. Field mice scamper over the moor, a whimbrel whistles in the marshes, ptarmigan busy themselves building nests among the tussocks, a honeybee growls in the moss, and plovers wait to be caught. Everything is greener and bluer, larger and fatter than he has ever seen before.

Then a fox barks from the stony ground at the mouth of the valley.

"Argh, argh!"

Skugga-Baldur pricks his ears at the call.

There's no mistaking the scent; it's a vixen in heat. Lust burns in his eyes, he puts his best paw forward and sets off down the fair valley; he will be the first to reach her.

It is spring before the days of man.

IV

(MARCH 23, 1883)

Brekka in the Dale, March 23, 1883

My dear friend,

Forgive me for replying so late to your last letter, but various things have happened in this part of the world since New Year's. They would not be thought particularly newsworthy in your world, but they are considered quite something here: a woman died, and a man was lost.

Yes, my Abba is dead. It happened on the fourth day of the New Year; she had a peaceful passing and was composed in her death. I have missed her a great deal, which is not to be wondered at, since I have had her by me all these years. She was not old, maybe thirty, which I gather is common with people of her sort. It was as if she aged more rapidly than I myself; she had turned gray and was becoming a little forgetful lately. Now, of course, you will ask yourself whether she received your feather. She did so, and it gave her much joy. She thought it quite something to possess the feather of a Danish cygnet, indeed she knew Herr Andersen's stories well—and she put it in her book straightaway on Christmas night.

I thank you also for my part. You are well versed in the French poets, though you are of the opinion that they cannot write, n'est-ce pas? Mallarmé affects me like a flowering cherry tree reflected in an eye, a scented handkerchief, or a dragonfly settling on the shoulder of a swimmer in a smooth river. Well, well, there you can see in black and white what a great inspiration he is!

A man was lost, I wrote, and I shall not keep you any longer in suspense over that news. It is the parson of Botn who has vanished, Reverend Baldur Skuggason, brother of Valdimar "Bollocks," who danced with the lamppost at the Leather Trousers. He was seized by the wild notion, foolish man, of rushing off on a fox hunt in the mountains, although it was the depths of winter and everyone knew that a great blizzard was in the offing. (An old cat scratched itself on New Year's Eve, and that means fearsome gales; this is the sort of "meteorologia" we practice here.) That is to say, he has not been seen since and it does not take a lively imagination to guess what has become of him.

People believe that this will result in a review of the living conditions of country priests. Reverend Baldur monopolized all foxhole work here in the parish to eke out his income, as the skins fetch a high price.

Certainly things have come to a pretty pass if priests have begun to throw away their lives on foxhunting, from purest penury.

"Good riddance" is all I have to say concerning the disappearance of Reverend Baldur; I thought him a terrible stupidus.

Abba means: Hafdís.
Itza means: God.
Itza ha-am means: God wills.
Itza um means: God may not.
Itz-umba uba-hara means: God's light, the sun
    or soul.
Ufa-hara ho-fakk means: the moon.
Ut-da-da ho-fakk means: the stars.
Iff-itz means: light.
Fuffa huya means: angels.
Iffa ku-ku means: heaven.
Itza i-addiga means: God knows all.
Otzina-maeya means: Christmas.
Itza ro-ro means: Jesus.
Otzina-huya means: Easter.
Otzina-mortha means: Sunday.
Avv-avv means: talk.
Ko-ko means: sing.
Andha ha-am ko-ko means: let us sing.
Umm avv-avv means: doesn't want to talk.

Umra means: don't know.

Amh-amh means: beautiful, good.

Offo-ker means: ugly.

Futzu means: man.

Hall-hall means: girl.

Fuffa-ro means: child.

Furru means: person.

Mamba means: bird.

Morthana-huya means: day.

Ho-fakk means: night.

Sa-odo means: the sea.

Fadi-fad means: rain.

Huyera means: snow.

Mah-mah means: summer.

Mah-mah huyera means: winter.

Ka means: fire.

Faff-faff means: priest.

Kondura means: king.

Tampa means: clothes.

Umph Abba's means: Hafdís's box.

Fifi-pupu means: hymn.

Pupu means: darkness.

Ibo means: sleep.

Here you have "Abba's Dictionary"; this is how she
spoke when I found her. As you see, there are a number
of biblical terms there, which supports my belief about

who she was . . . no, I won't be silent about what I know with certainty of Hafdís's origins. I have no secrets from you; you will keep them to yourself. I can always trust you, my good friend and master.

So it was that in late February we Dale folk were afflicted with one of the unluckiest men in Iceland; Solvi Helgason, vagabond and jack-of-all-trades. He slid on his skis from farm to farm, scrounging food in return for drawing people's likenesses, mending woodwork, or passing on gossip from other districts. This four-eyes knocked on my door too, and stayed here a week. I found out that he is clever with his paints and full of common sense. He did not bore me; but Solvi is damaged in mind and body, and this was the work of men.

Then one evening it so happened that he began to talk about Abba, calling her Laufey—it was I who gave her the name of Hafdís, saying she was Jón's daughter, which means no more than "Icelander's daughter"— but I could tell from his speech that he was sincere. He said he had found her abandoned on the Kjolur mountain track; she was seven years old at the time, he thought. She spent three seasons on the road with him, until he traced her family and was able to return her to her father's house. During the time that Abba was traveling with Solvi, he made her a coffin from precious driftwood that he had found by the Horn. When he mentioned this I knew he was telling the truth, because he could even describe two Latin inscriptions found in Abba's coffin; indeed, it was he who had written them.

Many years later Solvi came back to the farm where Laufey lived. Everything was in a fearful state: the mother had killed herself with poison and the father had sold the girl to some foreign sailors, while he himself was on his way to study for the priesthood. This wretched man was Baldur Skuggason, then deacon of Hofdi parish; in exchange for his twelve-year-old daughter he had received a front-loading rifle and a bag of shot.

Now you see why I speak so coldly of him above. But, dear me, how full of grief and sorrow this letter of mine has become; indeed, please forgive my tediousness.

Apropos! If you happen to pass down Kronprinsessegade, would you be so kind as to look in on Auntie Perch and order two pounds of Breakfast Blend and eight ounces of Darjeeling? I have an account and they send it to me. No, I don't intend to drink it alone. I "inherited" one of the priest's servants. His name is Hálfdán Atlason; he is simpleminded but hardworking, and sips enough tea to compete with the English House of Lords.

Please send my regards to your mother. I hope she likes the blend: thyme, dropwort, lady's bedstraw, and birch leaf. Let me know if you require more, there's plenty of choice in Iceland's natural pharmacy.

Farewell for now, my dearest Brynjulfsson, may good luck follow you—ad urnam.

Your affectionate friend and confidant on the limits of "the habitable world,"

Fridrik B.

Postscriptum: Again, please forgive me for such a dreary letter. I promise to do better next time, when I shall make sure to have a drop first! (The enclosed picture is by Solvi; it apparently shows the Devil shoving the highly esteemed governor up his a–e.)

Au revoir!

F.

A NOTE ABOUT THE AUTHOR

SJÓN is the author of, among other works, *From the Mouth of the Whale* and *The Whispering Muse*. Born in Reykjavík in 1962, he is an award-winning novelist, poet, and playwright, and his novels have been translated into twenty-five languages. He is the president of the Icelandic PEN Centre and chairman of the board of Reykjavík UNESCO City of Literature. Also a lyricist, he has written songs for Björk, including for her most recent project, *Biophilia*, and was nominated for an Oscar for the lyrics he cowrote (with Lars von Trier) for *Dancer in the Dark*. He lives in Reykjavík.

A NOTE ABOUT THE TRANSLATOR

VICTORIA CRIBB lived in Iceland for a number of years, working as a translator, journalist, and publisher. She has translated the works of Sjón, Gyrðir Elíasson, and Arnaldur Indriðason, and is currently studying for a Ph.D. in Old Icelandic literature at the University of Cambridge.